Postman Pat's Rainy Day was first published in 1983 by
André Deutsch Limited
Text Copyright © 1983 John Cunliffe
Illustrations © 1983 Celia Berridge and Ivor Wood

Postman Pat to the Rescue was first published in 1986 by
André Deutsch Limited
Text Copyright © 1986 John Cunliffe
Illustrations © 1986 Celia Berridge and Ivor Wood

Postman Pat's Thirsty Day and *Postman Pat Goes Sledging*
were first published in 1984 by André Deutsch Limited
Text Copyright © 1984 John Cunliffe
Illustrations © 1984 Celia Berridge and Ivor Wood

Postman Pat's Secret was first published in 1982 by
André Deutsch Limited
Text Copyright © 1982 John Cunliffe
Illustrations © 1982 Celia Berridge and Ivor Wood

Postman Pat and the Mystery Thief was first published in 1981 by
André Deutsch Limited
Text Copyright © 1981
Illustrations © 1981 Celia Berridge and Ivor Wood

This omnibus edition published in this format in 1991 by
Treasure Press
Michelin House
81 Fulham Road
London SW3 6RB

ISBN 1 85051 684 7

Printed in Hong Kong

MY FAVOURITE POSTMAN PAT STORIES

Written by John Cunliffe
Illustrated by Celia Berridge
From the original television designs by Ivor Wood

TREASURE PRESS

Postman Pat's
Rainy Day

"What a nasty day," said Pat.

He was driving his post-office van along Greendale, and it was raining. It had rained and rained for days and days, and it seemed that it would never stop. It rained so hard that the drops bounced off the road, and made big puddles. The rain banged on the roof of the van and rattled on the windows. In the fields, the sheep huddled behind the walls. Jess looked out at the rain with drooping whiskers – he hated wet days.

"What a day," said Pat. "It'll be wet letters and wet everything."

It was still raining when he reached the village post-office.

"What weather!" said Mrs. Goggins. "And just look at these letters!"

She had a warm fire in the back-room and she had clipped the letters to string washing-lines, to dry.

"Imagine them getting so wet, just being posted – I don't know what people do with them; and then the ink starts to smudge, and you can't read the address. It's like a wet wash-day, but worse."

"Aye, I see what you mean," said Pat. "But never mind; they'll soon dry."

"And you'd best look out for floods up the valley, Pat. There's more rain forecast, you know. It's enough to cause a landslide."

"Don't you worry," said Pat. "I'll see that the post gets through. It'll take more than a bit of rain to stop me."

He gathered up the damp pile of letters and parcels. "I'll be on my way, then. Cheerio!"

When Pat stepped out into the street, he found that the rain had stopped, but the sky was full of black clouds. He delivered the village letters quickly, without getting wet, then set out along the country roads.

Splashing through deep puddles, squelching up muddy tracks, and plodging through farmyards deep in mud, Pat was on his way. But who was this, standing at the roadside, soaking wet, and covered in black mud?

"Good heavens, it's Peter Fogg," said Pat, "but whatever's happened to him?"
He stopped to find out.

"It's this blooming rain," said Peter. "My old tractor bogged down in the bottom meadow. It's half-flooded down there! Then I slipped in the mud, up to my ears."

"You look as if you've had a bath in it," said Pat.

"I just about have," said Peter. "I'm off for some dry clothes, then I'll get the new tractor to pull the old one out."

"Good luck!" said Pat. "I think it's fairing up, now. Cheerio!"

When Pat reached the village school, some of the children were peering out to see if the rain had stopped. Charlie Pringle ran out for the letters.

"Hello, Charlie," said Pat. "Where's Bill Thompson, then?"

"He's off school to-day. They say there's flooding up at Thompson Ground. He'll be helping to get the sheep in."

"Well, don't drop the letters – they've already had one wetting," said Pat. The other children came out whilst they were talking, and now they were having a great time, jumping over puddles and in puddles and sailing paper boats.

"It's nice to see someone *enjoying* the rain," thought Pat. But time was getting on, and he must be on his way.

At Greendale Farm, Pat saw Peter Fogg again, looking much better after a good wash and a change of clothes. Peter showed Pat Mr. Pottage's new tractor with its bulldozer blade fitted.

"That'll shift anything," he said. Pat was impressed.

The next call was at the church. The Reverend Timms was having trouble with the rain, too.

"Good day, Pat," said the Reverend. "The rain rains on the just and the unjust."

"Good heavens!" said Pat. There were buckets and bowls and basins dotted about all over the church, with water drip-dripping into each one.

The drips kept falling in different places, so that the Reverend Timms had to keep moving the buckets and basins and bowls to catch them. He was dodging about all over the church, trying to keep up with the drops.

"The church roof isn't what it was," he said. "I think we will have to have an Appeal."

"I'll ask Ted Glen to bring his ladders, and have a look at that roof," said Pat. "He'll be able to fix it, I'm sure."

"Oh, thank you, Pat. That would be a *great* help. Just leave the letters on the pulpit; there are no drips there. Goodbye!"

"Goodbye!" called Pat.

Just along the road, Pat met Sam Waldron, with his mobile-shop.

"Take it steady, Pat," said Sam. "The roads are flooding further up the valley."

"Oh, the old van'll get me through," said Pat. He stopped to chat for a few minutes, and bought a bunch of bananas from Sam. Jess was glad to stay in the van, to keep out of the wet. He put his head out of the window to see what Pat was doing; a large raindrop fell right on his nose, and made him sneeze. Poor Jess!

They were getting into the hills, when they saw Mrs. Thompson standing in the road, waving them to stop.

"Hello, Mrs. Thompson, what's going on?" said Pat.

"There're terrible floods in the top fields, Pat, and the water's brought tons of earth down and blocked the road. Come and see."

Pat walked with her, down the hill and round the next bend in the road. A great pile of rocks and earth and mud lay right across the road and in the fields on both sides. Nothing could get past.

"Dear me," said Pat, "can't we telephone the village for help?"

"No – the lines are down."

"Can't we walk round it?"

"It's too dangerous with these floods; you could be buried if the land started to slip again."

They heard an engine coming along the road.

"Here comes Alf," said Mrs. Thompson, "he's going to try to get through with the tractor."

"Do you think he can do it?" said Pat.

"I'll have a jolly good try!" Alf shouted.

Off he went, at top speed, towards the pile of stones and earth. The engine roared and the wheels were spinning and skidding in the wet mud. The tractor climbed over the first of the rubble, and then there was a loud bang as its nose hit a large rock. It was stuck. Alf tried again and again, but it wouldn't move. It took him another ten minutes to back out of the mess and the tractor was damaged at the front.

"It's no good," said Alf. "We'll have to get help, somehow."

Then Bill came, with his model aeroplane.

"I've got a good idea," he said. "We can put a message on my plane and I can fly it across to Greendale Farm to get help."

"That is a good idea," said Pat. "Clever lad – we'll send an air-mail letter."

So Pat wrote a note – "ROAD BLOCKED AT THOMPSON GROUND. PLEASE SEND HELP. PAT."

He tied it to the plane with a bit of Alf's binder-twine. Bill stood on a little hill, where he could just see the distant chimneys of Greendale Farm, and twiddled his radio-controls. He started the engine and the aeroplane flew up into the sky. Bill steered it carefully and it flew away, towards Greendale Farm. "Away she goes!" cried Pat. "*That's* better than a van. I wonder if I could swop mine for a helicopter?"

"I think it's landed now," said Bill.

The Thompsons went off to see to the sheep, whilst Pat sat on the wall to wait. It seemed ages since the plane had gone. He was just thinking it must have crashed, when he heard a powerful engine coming up the road on the other side of the blockage. It was Peter Fogg on the new tractor, with the bulldozer-blade.

"Got your letter!" he shouted.

He drove into the rubble. The bulldozer-blade pushed the earth and stones to one side of the road, with a loud grinding and screeching of metal and stones and earth. The huge wheels bit into the ground and pushed the tractor forward. He was through!

"Thanks, Peter!" shouted Pat.

"Right you are!" shouted Peter.

When Sam Waldron came along, in his mobile-shop, there was just enough room for him to get through. Pat followed in his van; he was glad to be on his way again.

Pat called at farms and houses all along the valley, delivering letters and cards and parcels. He told everyone he met about the landslide at Thompson Ground and how Peter Fogg had come to the rescue. When he saw Ted Glen by the road, mending a wall, he remembered something else, and stopped to talk to him.

"Can you go and have a look at the church roof, Ted? The Reverend has the church full of buckets."

"I'll pop along when I've finished this wall," said Ted. "Bloomin' rain; it makes no end o' work."

Miss Hubbard came past on her bike; she was on her way to choir practice.

"I'd turn back if I were you," said Pat, "or you might have to swim home."

"Swim?" said Miss Hubbard. "It'll take more than a drop of rain to stop me."
And on she went.

"I'll be on my way, too," said Pat. "Cheerio!"

As Pat wound his way along the valley, it looked like rain again; but there was a warm fireside to look forward to, when all the letters had been delivered.

Postman Pat
to the Rescue

The day had started cloudy in Greendale, but as Pat set out along the valley, on the way to the village post-office, the sun began to come out. Pat's red van went twisting and turning along the windy roads. He went through Greendale Forest, where all the birds were singing. He went round the sharp corner by Garner Hall, then put his brakes on, hard.

There was a big van almost blocking the road. It was Sam's mobile shop.
   "It's going to be a tight squeeze," said Pat. He drove on to the grass at the edge of the road. Sam popped his head round the corner of his van. He waved Pat on.
   "Come on!" he shouted. "You've got plenty of room!" Pat wasn't so sure. He edged slowly alongside Sam's van.

"Left a bit!" called Sam. "A bit more. Left . . . left . . . right . . . straighten up . . . keep going, you're OK. Come on, come on . . . that's it."
   Pat stopped by Sam's van, and opened his window.
   "Hello, Sam," he said. "Thanks for seeing me through. Could you give Mrs. Atkinson her letters please?"
   "Right-o, Pat. Mind how you go. Cheerio!"

Sam went off with Mrs. Atkinson's letters and groceries. Pat tried to drive away, but the van didn't move.

"Oh dear," said Pat, putting his head out of the window. He could see the wheel whizzing round and sinking down into the muddy ground. "I think we're stuck."

He revved the engine again, but the wheel just went deeper in.

"Now we are stuck. It's all that rain. It's made the ground boggy."

Sam came back.

"Hello, Pat! Still here?"

"Yes, I am," said Pat, "I'm stuck."

"Don't worry," said Sam. "I'll give Pete Fogg a shout as I go past – he can tow you out with his tractor."

"Thanks, Sam. Cheerio!"

Pat sat on the wall, to wait for Peter Fogg to come. Up on the hillside, he could see Alf and Dorothy Thompson busy with their hay-making. He could see the sheep and their lambs running and skipping in the green fields by the river.

Peter came at last. Pat was glad to see him.

"Hello, Peter," he said, "can you tow me out, please? My van's stuck in the mud."

"Easy," said Peter. "Sam told me you needed help. I'll just back up."

Peter turned his tractor in a gateway, then backed up until it was in front of Pat's van. Then he got his tow-rope out.

"Now then – just tie it on there," said Peter.

"Right-o," said Pat, tying it to a special bracket under the front bumper. Peter climbed on to the tractor again, and started the engine.

"Right?" he called.

"Yes, all ready," said Pat.

Peter drove slowly forward, until the rope was tight. He put more and more power on, until Pat's van began to ease out of the mud.

Soon it was on the hard road again. Peter took the rope off. Pat started his engine and waved to Peter.

"Bye! Thanks a lot!"

"Cheerio, Pat!"

Pat was on his way again.

When he arrived at the post-office, Mrs. Goggins said, "Morning, Pat. You're a bit late to-day."

So he told her all about how he had been stuck in the mud, and had to wait for Peter Fogg to come and pull him out. She showed him the Pencaster Gazette.

"Look," she said, "there's a picture of Major Forbes' bull. It's won first prize in the county show. Isn't it a magnificent beast? Have you seen it?"

"No," said Pat, "and I don't think I want to either."

"There's a letter for the major, so you might meet the bull: better keep a sharp look out."

"I'd run a mile if I saw it," said Pat. "Cheerio!"

Pat hadn't gone far, when he saw Ted Glen waving to him to stop.

"Some fool's left a gate open," he said, when Pat stopped. "I'll bet it's those campers. The sheep have got into the clover-field. It'll kill them if they eat too much. Can you give me a hand to drive them out?"

"Yes, of course I will," said Pat. "I used to work on a farm when I was a lad. Have they gone far, then?"

"You can see them up there. They have spread out a bit. "We'd better get after them."

The sheep were spread across the hillside, busily munching the clover that was so bad for them.

"You go that way, I'll go this," said Ted.

"Right!" said Pat.

What a time they had, catching those naughty sheep! The sheep ran all over the place. They jumped over walls and gates, dodged round trees and bushes, and hid in the long grass.

By the time Pat and Ted had chased them back into their own field, and closed the gate, they were hot and out of breath.

"Phew, that was warm work," said Ted.

"What's that funny noise?" said Pat.

"Hey up, it's that bull!" shouted Ted. "Run!"

They ran all down the steep hill, and jumped over the wall at the bottom. Ted said, "Ouch!" as he landed with a thump on the grass at the side of the road.

"What's up, Ted?" said Pat.

Ted could not stand up, and his leg seemed to be twisted.

"It's my ankle," said Ted. "By gum, it does hurt! Ouch, I can't get up. I think it's broken."

"Now what are we going to do?" said Pat. "You can't sit here till it gets better. I'd better go and get Dr. Gilbertson from the village. Won't be long!"

Pat drove away in his van, to Dr. Gilbertson's house. He gave the doctor her letters, then he told her about Ted's broken ankle.

"Oh dear, my car's in Pencaster being serviced," said Dr. Gilbertson.

"Then I'll take you in my van," said Pat.

So Dr. Gilbertson brought her bag and rode in the van. She sat in Jess's place, with Jess on her knee.

Ted was so glad to see the doctor. She soon bandaged his ankle up, with quite a bit of oooh-ing and ow-ing from Ted. It wasn't broken, just badly sprained.

"Try not to put too much weight on it, now," said the doctor.

Pat's walking-stick came in handy to help Ted to hobble to the van.

"Thanks, Pat," said Ted.

"You'll have to ride amongst the letters," said Pat.

"Easy, now."

Ted climbed in the back.

Jess rode back again on Dr. Gilbertson's knee.
They took the doctor home. Then they took Ted home.
Ted was glad to get home.
"You all right, now?" said Pat.
"I'll manage," said Ted. "Thanks for helping."
"Cheerio!"
"Bye!"

Pat was on his way again. He still had a lot of letters and parcels to deliver. He met Alf and Dorothy along the road, on their tractor.

"Hello, Alf!" called Pat.

"Hello, Pat," said Alf. "Thanks for getting the sheep back. It's the same thing every year – gates left open all over – we'll have to have words with them campers, won't we, Dot?"

Pat went on his way.

"What a morning, Jess! Rounding sheep up, dodging a bull, fetching the doctor – and now we're late with all this post. We'll have to get a move on, this afternoon."

Postman Pat's
Thirsty Day

It was another hot day in Greendale...a *very* hot day.
In the fields, the sheep looked for any patch of shade – under a tree, behind a wall.
They gathered there, panting, in their woolly coats.

"It's a real scorcher to-day," said Pat to Jess, as they drove along. "Phew, I'm thirsty already."
The lakes were drying up. The stream was down to a trickle.

At the village post-office, Mrs. Goggins was outside, looking out for Pat, and trying to get cool.

"Morning Pat!" she called. "Isn't it hot! *And* we're going to be without water to-day."

"I know," said Pat, "the lake's really low and they're going to turn the water off this morning. Whatever will we do?"

"Well, I've filled the kettle and two pans," said Mrs. Goggins.

They went into the post-office. Mrs. Goggins took a bottle of lemonade out of the fridge. She said, "But they can't turn the lemonade off. There you are, Pat, have a drink before you go."

"Mmmmm...lovely," said Pat, "thank you, just what I need...My, that's good...that's much better. Well, I'd better be on my way. Thanks for the drink! Cheerio!"

Pat collected his letters and parcels. There was a parcel marked FRAGILE, for Granny Dryden.

"Now take good care of that," said Mrs. Goggins. "It looks like something from that catalogue of hers."

"I will," said Pat. "I ordered a watch from her. It might be that. Cheerio!"

Pat was on his way.

He began his round with the village letters. Along the winding streets, through narrow passageways, in and out of cottage gardens he went, and everyone was pleased to see him.

He met Granny Dryden out shopping, and told her about the parcel. "It's in the van," he said. "I'll pop in with it later." Then he told her about the water being cut off.

"Well, it's a pity the old pump isn't working," she said. "There were plenty of dry summers in my young days, and, do you know, that pump *never* dried up, not once!"

"I wonder," said Pat. "I wonder if Ted Glen could mend it? I must ask him. He can fix just about anything."

Pat tried the rusty handle of the pump, as he passed it, but it wouldn't move. He finished the village letters, then set out for the farms in his van.

At Greendale Farm, the water was already off. Peter Fogg was winding buckets of water up from the old well, to get water for the cows. Katy and Tom were helping to carry the water to the trough.

"Hello," said Pat. "You still have water in the well, then? Let's have a look."
He bent over to peer into the mossy depths. He could hear water splashing and dripping, but it was too dark and deep to see. He bent further, then – "Ooooops!" – his hat slipped off and dropped into the well.

"Oh dear," said Pat, "I'll never see that again."

"I wonder if I can fish it out with the hook," said Peter. "Let's try."

He lowered the hook without the bucket on it, and swung it about at the bottom. When he wound it up again, Pat's hat was on it, dripping wet, and trailing strands of water-weed.

"It will be nice and cool, anyway," said Peter.

"Thanks," said Pat. "Now I mustn't drop your letters down the well."

"No," said Peter. "Thanks, Pat – and would you mind dropping off a drum of water for George Lancaster? He hasn't got a well, or a spring, so he must be desperate for water by now."

"Certainly," said Pat. "We'll be going past his road-end. Cheerio!"

High in the hills, at Intake Farm, George Lancaster had no water at all. He was very glad to see the big plastic drum of water in the back of Pat's van.

"Special delivery," said Pat. "A parcel of water. There's no address on it, but it looks pretty dry here, so I think it must be for you."

"Thanks, Pat," said George. "You've saved my life. We've dried out completely up here."

Pat remembered to call at Ted Glen's workshop to ask if Ted could mend the old village pump.

"Well, I don't know," said Ted, "That pump hasn't been used since I was a boy. The works may be all rusted away. But Granny Dryden's lived all her life in Greendale, and she knows a thing or two, so she could be right about that pump. Besides, my water's been off all morning, and I'm thirsty, so it's worth a try. I'll just get my tools. Leave it to me!"

At Thompson Ground, Dorothy Thompson was enjoying a cup of tea, when Pat called with a letter.

"Hello," said Pat, "isn't your water off? Everyone else's is."

"No, we have a spring," said Mrs. Thompson. "It comes out of the hillside just above the house. It's never been known to dry up – not since grandad was a boy, anyway, and that was a very long time ago."

"You *are* lucky," said Pat, and he told her about the village pump. "I wonder how Ted's getting on?"

Down in the village, Ted was very busy. He was hard at work on that old pump, and a crowd had gathered to watch and cheer him on. Mrs. Goggins brought him a pot of tea to keep him going.

Miss Hubbard brought him a frying-pan that needed mending. The Reverend Timms promised to say a prayer for rain, at Evensong. Alf Thompson said there was nothing like a really good spring. But Ted just kept on working.

He carefully took everything to pieces. He put oil and grease on the rusty bearings, and cleaned all the rust away. He hammered a bent rod until it was ruler-straight. He fitted a new washer. He cleaned fifty years of rubbish out of the pipes – old twigs and leaves, newspapers, dirty rags, a dead mouse. At last, he put the pump together again. He tightened everything up, and screwed the top on.

"Now then; let's see," he said. He worked the handle up and down. Nothing happened. "It's gone dry," someone said. He tried again.

There was a gurgle deep in the pipes. Again. A spurt of rusty water gushed out, wetting everyone! "Hurrah!" they all cheered.

Ted went on pumping. The water ran rusty-golden for a time, then it came clean and clear. Pat arrived in time to see it.

"I knew you'd do it," he said. "I just knew you would. Granny Dryden *will* be pleased. I'll take her some water, to celebrate."

Everyone queued up to fill their cans and buckets, and thank Ted. Jess came for a drink, and had an unexpected shower.

When Pat called on Granny Dryden, he told her all about how Ted had mended the pump, and gave her a can of water with her parcel. She was delighted.

"I'll have to come and see for myself," she said.

She opened the parcel. It was the new digital-watch that Pat had ordered from her catalogue.

"That's good," said Pat. "I'll always be on time, now. I'll bring the money to-morrow. Cheerio! Look after yourself!"

Pat had kept a can of water for himself. Jess kept a sharp eye on it, all the way home. He didn't want another wetting, no matter *how* hot it was.

Postman Pat's
Secret

It was a special day for Pat. He wouldn't tell anyone why it was a special day, because it was his secret, a secret that he had kept for many years. Pat sang as he drove along the valley; it was a happy day, too. Jess sat beside him, and twitched his whiskers.

"Now, young Jess, don't you give my secret away," said Pat. Jess promised not to say one word about it.

When Pat arrived at the village post-office, Mrs. Goggins was looking out for him and she was looking very pleased about something.

"Hello, Pat," she said, "there's such a lot of post to-day!"

Pat didn't look too pleased, until he saw that much of it was for him. But who could be writing all these letters to Pat? One had a drawing of a cat on it, and the writing looked suspiciously like Katy Pottage's.

"Why don't you open them?" said Mrs. Goggins, "Then you'll know who sent them."

So Pat did.

What a surprise! They were all birthday-cards.

He stood them in a row along the counter. There was one from every person on his round. He was very pleased, after all, but how did everyone know that it was his birthday to-day? *That* was his secret, and now it was no longer a secret at all.

"How did they know?" said Mrs. Goggins. "Well, *I* didn't tell them and that's all I'm saying, except – Happy Birthday, Pat, and many happy returns."

Pat bought six chocolate kittens, then gathered up all his cards, and the day's letters, and went on his way.

At Greendale Farm, the twins were looking out for Pat, and sang "Happy Birthday To You", when he came in with the letters, and Mrs. Pottage joined in, too.

Pat showed them all his cards. Then Mrs. Pottage whisked a cloth off the table, and there was a birthday-cake, with an icing-sugar post-office van on it, and pink letters saying BIRTHDAY GREETINGS TO POSTMAN PAT. And there was a sugar-mouse for Jess.

"But how did you know it was my birthday?" said Pat.

"We're not telling," said Mrs. Pottage. "It's a secret."

"It *was* a secret," sighed Pat. "But, all the same...thank you very much; it is a lovely cake."

Then he was off on his way.

"Goodbye!"

The church was the next stop, as there were some letters for the Reverend Timms.

"And here's something for you, on your birthday," said the Reverend. He gave Pat a Bible, bound in leather.

"That's very kind of you," said Pat, "but how did you know it was my birthday?"

"He who reads shall learn," said the Reverend Timms.

"Oh?" said Pat, puzzled. How could the Bible tell the secret of his birthday? He couldn't guess.

When Jess saw it, he wondered if it was a sugar-bible.

Pat drove away, up the winding hilly roads, and arrived at Thompson Ground just in time for a cup of tea. Mrs. Thompson was just looking at Pat's birthday-cards, when Alf came in.

"Hello, Pat," he said, "and a very happy birthday!"
He gave Pat a walking-stick, with a curly horn handle, that he'd made himself.
"That'll be good for keeping dogs off," he said.
"Thank you," said Pat, "it will be very useful, but *how* did you know it was my birthday?"
"Oh, you'll find out for yourself. Just keep your eyes open," said Alf, smiling. "You're quite a famous postman, you know."

"Whatever does he mean?" thought Pat, as he waved goodbye to the Thompsons. He was getting more and more puzzled, and his van was filling up with presents. Jess didn't like the sheep's horn on the walking-stick; he thought it might butt him when he wasn't looking.

When Pat called on Granny Dryden, she gave him a woolly vest that she had knitted specially. It looked *very* itchy!

And Miss Hubbard gave him a steering-wheel cover, made of red velvet, to keep his hands warm in winter.

At Intake Farm, George Lancaster gave Pat two dozen eggs, all different colours, laid by his prize hens.

When Pat met Sam Waldron, along the road, with his mobile-shop, Sam gave him a big box of strawberries, and carton of cream.

Pat called late at the village school because they'd all been away for the morning, on a visit to Pencaster Castle. They were ready for Pat, though, all the same. They sang him two songs that they had been practising, and gave him a big model of his van that they had made specially.

Pat had presents for them – a chocolate kitten each – to say thank you for all their cards. How pleased they were! But when he asked how they knew about his birthday, the children smiled, pressed fingers to their lips and said nothing.

Pat must get on his way home now. He did not want to be late, because he knew his wife would have a special birthday meal ready for him. The day's round was finished, and Pat's last job was to empty the letter-box.

Peter Fogg came along on his tractor, and stopped for a chat. Pat told him about how everyone knew his birthday.

"Don't you know why?" said Peter, laughing.

"I certainly do *not*!" said Pat.

Peter pulled a newspaper out of his pocket. It was the Pencaster Gazette.

"Have a look at this," he said.

Pat was amazed. There was a piece all about him, headed POSTMAN OF THE YEAR. It told the story of his work, and how he helped everyone he met, where he had been to school, where he was born, and *when* he was born!

"*Well*," said Pat, "so that's how everyone knew. I'll be *bothered*, these newspaper people, they find everything out." He was cross and pleased, at the same time.

"Keep it as a souvenir," said Peter.

"Thanks," said Pat, "and that surely is my last present to-day."

"What next?" thought Jess. "We'll never get home at this rate."

But they were on their way home this time.

"I wonder when *my* birthday is?" said Jess to himself. "It's such a good secret that even *I* don't know! I wish I could find it in the paper, then *I* could have cards and presents. Never mind, there'll be a good dinner waiting for me, and that's as good as a birthday any time."

"What a strange day," said Pat. "We've finished up with a van full of letters and parcels."

And off they went home; but Jess didn't have his usual cat-nap – he wanted to keep an eye on that ram's horn, just in case it tried anything funny.

Postman Pat
and the Mystery Thief

One sunny morning, Pat was hurrying along the road with a van full of letters and parcels for the people of Greendale. Over a hill and round a corner, he had to jam his brakes on, because the road was full of sheep.

Jess wanted to know what was going on; he popped his head out of the open window to have a look. Just then, a big ram, with great curly horns, pushed up to the van, right in Jess's face! What a fright they both had! Jess jumped into his basket and Pat stroked him, to cheer him up. Peter Fogg was driving his sheep across the road, with

his dogs, Bess and Ben. He opened a gate, and the sheep went into the field, baa-ing and following their leader. Peter waved as he fastened the gate and Pat went on his way.

But he soon had to stop again – this time for a herd of cows. The cows walked slowly by; they never hurried. Alf Thompson was walking behind them. He waved his stick, and shouted, "Get up, then!" but it made no difference; the cows mooed, stopped to munch the roadside grasses, and took their time. The road was clear at last. Alf Thompson waved to Pat, and Pat was on his way again.

When Pat stopped at the village school, he saw Charlie Pringle carrying a bunch of flowers.

"What lovely flowers," said Pat.

"They're for our spring display," said Charlie. "We're all bringing something. Look; here comes Lucy – and Katy and Tom."

They all had something special. Lucy Selby had brought a basket of eggs and Tom Pottage a box of day-old chicks. They all showed Pat what they had brought.

Then Pat was off again, away up the steep hills and winding roads. In and out of farmyards he went, delivering cards and letters and parcels. There was an urgent packet of medicines for Mr. Forsyth, the vet, and a letter from the football-pools, for George Lancaster.

"I wonder if he's had a win," said Pat, but George was out on the fells, so he couldn't ask him. It was just about dinner-time and Pat was on the hill above Thompson Ground.

"What a nice place for a picnic," he said. So he parked his van on the grass by the roadside and Jess jumped out, glad to stretch his legs. Pat locked the van. They found a sunny place to sit in the field, with a grassy slope to lean against. Several of Mrs. Thompson's hens were scratching about along the hedges. From this high hill

Pat could see the whole valley, with the Thompsons' farm on the steep hillside just below where he was sitting. Pat thought he could almost peep down the chimney and see Mrs. Thompson putting the kettle on the fire. Jess was thinking about Pat's sandwich-box and hoping there was a tin of sardines in it.

Pat placed the box on the grass, with his keys neatly beside it, so as not to forget them. Then he opened the box. Jess was in luck; there was a whole tin of sardines to share with Pat, as well as sandwiches, an apple, a yoghurt and a big slice of cherry-cake. They began to eat, but it was so warm in the sun that both Pat and Jess began to feel sleepy. They closed their eyes. Mrs. Thompson's hens were not a bit sleepy. They had spotted Pat's food, too. They pecked their way nearer and nearer to Pat and Jess and the open sandwich box.

Then, a noise wakened Pat. He sat up and blinked. Two hens were running away with sandwiches in their beaks and a third was pecking at the yoghurt. Pat shouted, jumped up, and chased the hens, but he couldn't catch them. Jess chased another into the hedge. Pat ran back to the sandwich-box just in time to see another cheeky hen running away with his keys in its beak. He chased her down the hill, but she spread her wings and flew into a tree.

"I must get my keys," said Pat. "I cannot open my van or deliver my letters without them! Dear me, it's a long time since I climbed a tree, but I'd better try."

Jess stretched his paws up the trunk of the tree, digging his claws in and glaring up at the hen. He could easily climb, but he knew that he couldn't get down again. The cheeky hen sat on a high branch, with the keys in its beak, looking down at Pat and Jess. Pat began to climb, nearer and nearer to the hen.

He was just reaching out to grab the keys, when the hen dropped them into a hollow in the tree and flew off to the farmyard with a loud squawk. Now Pat had to climb higher, to search for his keys. He put his foot on a rotten branch. Crack! It gave way and Pat and branch came tumbling down. Pat landed in the middle of a prickly bush. It broke his fall, but it scratched and prickled him all over. Mrs Thompson had heard the commotion and came out to see what was going on. She pulled Pat out of the bush and pulled the prickles out of him. He told her all about the thieving hens.

"Dear me," said Mrs. Thompson, "that one must think she's a magpie, or some such; they're the ones for taking anything shiny. We'd better get a ladder and see if we can find your keys."

"There'll be no post for the dale, unless we do," said Pat.

"That won't do," said Mrs. Thompson, "specially when I'm expecting a letter from Auntie Jean, to say if she's coming for Easter."

So they went for the ladder and leaned it against the tree. Pat climbed up easily now. Whilst Mrs. Thompson held the ladder, Pat looked amongst the branches and found the hollow where the hen had dropped his keys. He found a lot of other things there, too.

"It's like a nest," he said; 'a magpie's nest."

He brought everything down to show Mrs. Thompson. There were all kinds of shiny things; bits of glass, wire, a milk-bottle top, buttons, a doll's eye and something larger among the bits and glittery pieces, as well as Pat's keys.

"That's my wedding-ring, that went missing last Easter, and I thought I'd lost it down the sink," cried Mrs. Thompson. "I *am* glad to see it again." She wiped it clean on her apron and put it on her finger. When they had put the ladder away, she said,

"My hens have stolen your sandwiches, so you'd better come and have some dinner with me – there's plenty to spare."

Pat was glad he'd lost his sandwiches when he saw what a good dinner Mrs. Thompson had cooked. So was Jess; he had a tasty plate of fish and a bowl of creamy milk. It was all much better than the best of sandwiches. Mrs. Thompson was happy, too, to see her ring shining on her finger once more.

It was time to be on the way and Pat said, "Goodbye," and "Thank you," to Mrs. Thompson. As they drove along, Pat's pocket jingled with all the shiny things he had found in the tree.

"Just fancy," he said, "a magpie-hen. Who ever heard of such a thing?"

Jess wondered what a magpie-cat would collect. Further along the road, they saw the mobile-shop and Pat stopped to have a chat with Sam Waldron. He told Sam the story of the magpie-hen.

"It had better keep away from my van," he said. "I wonder if that's where my tie-pin went?"

Pat showed him the hen's collection. There were no tie-pins among the glittery bits.

Pat went on his way. He had some letters for Miss Hubbard and he told her about the magpie-hen.

"Well," she said, "I lost a silver earring last month, and a hatpin. I wonder if they're up a tree somewhere?"

Pat showed her the glittery bits.

"That hen could have another hoard, in another tree," she said. "I must go and see Mrs. Thompson and have a good look."

Along by Garner Bridge, Pat met George Lancaster on his tractor and stopped to tell *him* about the thieving magpie-hen. George couldn't think of anything he'd lost, but he thought it made a good story.

"Well, but you might have won something," said Pat. "There's a letter for you from the pools."

"Is there, by Jove; I'll be off then," said George and sped away at top speed.

On the way home, Pat saw some real magpies and wondered if they had taught Mrs. Thompson's hens how to steal.

As for Jess, *he* was asleep.

Postman Pat
Goes Sledging

There was deep snow in Greendale.

Peter Fogg was out early. He had the snow-plough fitted to the big tractor, and he was clearing the snow from the roads. No one could get about until the roads were cleared, and the council snow-plough would be busy on the main roads around Pencaster.

Peter left a clear way behind him, and a little procession followed....
Postman Pat in his van;
Sam Waldron in his mobile-shop;
and Miss Hubbard on her bike.

The Reverend Timms was digging the snow from the vicarage path, and waved as they all went by.

At the village post-office, Mrs. Goggins was full of news.

"They do say there are ten-foot drifts up the top road, Pat, and here's an urgent parcel for George Lancaster. You'll never get up there to-day, you know, not with all this snow."

"Oh dear," said Pat, "but I'd better take it, just in case I can get through. I usually manage, somehow."

"Well, mind how you go, Pat. We don't want you getting buried in the snow like those poor sheep."

"Oh, I'll be all right. Cheerio!"

Pat was on his way, driving slowly along the slippery roads.

At Greendale Farm, the twins were waiting for Pat, with a pile of snowballs.
A snowball whizzed through the air, and hit Pat right on the nose.
"Oh, you young monkeys!" shouted Pat. "Two can play at that game."

He made a big snowball, and aimed at Tom's nose.
"Oh!"
Oh dear! Tom dodged. Pat was not a good shot and, just at that moment, Alf Thompson came out of the house. *Smack!* The snowball hit him right in the face.
"Oh, sorry, Mr. Thompson!" shouted Pat, "I didn't know you were there. I was aiming at the twins."

"That's all right," said Alf. "It's only a bit of fun. Now then, Pat, you'll have to stop here a bit. The road's blocked and Peter's stuck with his tractor in a big drift. We've come to try and dig it out. Can you give us a hand?"
"Certainly," said Pat.

He gave Mrs. Pottage her letters. Then he borrowed a spade and set out along
the snowy road with Alf and Ted Glen. When they came to the tractor, Peter was
already hard at work, digging out the high wall of snow.

They all joined in. It took a long time to make a big enough gap. Then Peter
started up the tractor and took a run at the snowdrift.

"Hurrah!" He was through.

Now Pat's van could get through, so off he went. He called at the vicarage with letters for the Reverend Timms, but Dr. Gilbertson came to the door.
"Come in, Pat," she said. "The Reverend's slipped on the ice and broken his leg. I've just finished bandaging him up. The ambulance will be coming for him, as soon as the roads are clear."

There was the Reverend, sitting with his leg propped up on a cushion, in splints and bandages. He cheered up when he saw Pat with his letters.
"Wasn't this a silly thing to do, Pat," he said. "And I was just going to take the parish magazine round too. *Now* what am I going to do?"

"Don't worry," said Pat. "I can take it with my letters. No trouble at all. I'll see they get through. Now you enjoy your letters, and rest that leg, and you'll soon be better. Cheerio!"

At Thompson Ground, Dorothy Thompson was out collecting the eggs.
"I hope you haven't any letters for anybody up the top road," she said.
"The snow's so bad that Peter had to turn back. The tractor just couldn't get up the hill. It was slipping all over the place."
    "Well, yes, I have a parcel for George, and it's marked URGENT," said Pat.
"What can I do? Perhaps I could walk it?"

"I have a better idea," said Alf. "We can go up on the old farm-sledge. I have to take some food up for the sheep, anyway."

"Well....it's a long time since I was on a sledge," said Pat doubtfully. Alf pulled the big sledge out of the barn.

"Here we are," he said, "we'll be all right on this."

"And you'd better take George some groceries," said Dorothy. "He'll be getting short, with being snowed up. Jess can stay by the fire, with me."

They loaded the sledge up, with bales of hay and a box of groceries, and off they went.

It was hard going uphill. Alf pulled and Pat pushed. When they came to a downhill stretch, they jumped on and rode, skimming over the frozen snow. That was *lovely!*

Alf's sheep were glad to see them. They gathered round in the snow, bleating. Alf untied the bales of hay, and spread the hay on the snow. The sheep ran to it with little bleats of joy. Then Alf and Pat pushed on to Intake Farm.

George's house was half buried in the snow. Pat knocked at the door.
"Hello!" he called. "Anybody in?"
There was no answer.
"George'll be out, seeing to *his* sheep," said Alf. "The door's sure to be open."
It was, so they left the parcel and the box of groceries on the kitchen table, with a note, on the back of an old envelope.

Now the sledge was empty, and it was downhill most of the way back.

"We'll have a fast ride home," said Alf. "Hold tight, Pat! Give us a push! Here we go!"

And off they went.

They whizzed across the fields, faster and faster. The snow was so deep that they went over the tops of the walls. They hit a bump, and over they went, tumbled and rolled in a deep drift of snow. They picked themselves up, found the sledge, climbed aboard, and off they went again. Pat hadn't enjoyed himself so much for years. Faster and faster, down the hill they went.

"How are we going to stop?" Pat shouted.

"I don't know!" shouted Alf. "Just hang on!"

Alf had forgotten how to stop a sledge, but they soon found out! Thompson Ground came into sight, and Alf steered for the yard.

They shot through the open gate, scattering hens in all directions, and straight into the barn. They crashed into a pile of hay bales, and fell off again, shouting and laughing. What a mess they were! They were covered in snow, bits of hay, and muck from the barn-floor. They staggered into the house like drunken scarecrows.

Jess was curled up on the rug in front of a warm fire. Dorothy had the kettle on. Alf and Pat cleaned themselves up, warmed themselves by the fire, and soon had a good hot mug of tea in their hands.

"My goodness – that *was* an exciting ride," said Pat. "But I'd better be on my way now. I still have some letters to deliver. Thanks for the ride and the tea. Come on, Jess, you'll have to leave that fire, now. Cheerio!"

The rest of Pat's round was in the valley, and the roads had been cleared and gritted by now.

"No more digging or sledging to-day," said Pat to Jess. "It'll take more than snow to stop us."

But Jess was curled up, fast asleep, and dreaming of that lovely warm fireside and Mrs. Thompson's woolly rug.